THE LOST YEARS OF MERLIN SAGA

T. A. BARRON

ACE BOOKS, NEW YORK

THE LOST YEARS OF MERLIN SAGA

An Ace Book / published by arrangement with
the author

PRINTING HISTORY
Ace edition / July 2002

Visit our website at
www.penguinputnam.com
Check out the ACE Science Fiction & Fantasy newsletter!

ISBN: 0-441-01019-9

ACE®
Ace Books are published by The Berkley Publishing Group,
a division of Penguin Putnam Inc.,
375 Hudson Street, New York, New York 10014.
ACE and the "A" design
are trademarks belonging to Penguin Putnam Inc.

PRINTED IN THE UNITED STATES OF AMERICA

10 9 8 7 6 5 4 3 2 1

contents

Introduction to *The Lost Years of Merlin* series
by T. A. Barron   vii

Biography of T. A. Barron   ix

Excerpt from *The Lost Years of Merlin*   1

Excerpt from *The Seven Songs of Merlin*   21

Excerpt from *The Fires of Merlin*   39

Excerpt from *The Mirror of Merlin*   53

Excerpt from *The Wings of Merlin*   69

The LEGENDARY
ISLE OF
FINCAYRA

strange peoples live here

L A N D S

where be the Otherworld well?

Slantos

caverns

The Shrouded Castle

EAGLES' CANYON

Dance of the Giants is prophesied

THE RUSTED PLAINS

ruins

Goblins' Encampment

Home of Cairpré

The Notch

THE DARK HILLS

be there treasures?

Town of the Bards

T'eilean and Garlatha

THE HAUNTED MARSH

Domnu's Lair the Galator may lie here

ruins

Ever mist surrounds the ISLE

INTRODUCTION

Everyone knows Merlin. Right? He is that wise old fellow who is the mentor of King Arthur, the sage of Camelot, and—for many people—the greatest wizard of all time.

And Merlin has surely stood the test of time! For over fifteen centuries, people have told stories about this intriguing character. Long, long ago—before the first Celtic tales were even written down—bards sang ballads about the wonders of the man called Merlin.

But what was he like *before* he became an exalted wizard? Before he grew up? What was he like when he was still young—too young to know about his glorious destiny? These are the questions that led me to write the five-book epic *The Lost Years of Merlin*. I started wondering about his life as a young man: his greatest struggles, his highest hopes, his darkest fears. And I started wondering what crucial events, what experiences, and what friends and enemies shaped the powerful Merlin we celebrate today.

Something else, too. I couldn't help but wonder why we knew so little about Merlin's youth. In the thousands of stories about him, ranging back across the centuries, only a tiny handful reveal anything at all about those early years. It almost seemed as if those years had been lost from time. Lost from the world of story and song.

Could it be, I asked myself, that Merlin *himself* was lost during those years? That he voyaged to a faraway land, where he had experiences so wondrous and so terrible that he vowed never to reveal them? Never, that is— until now. And so begins the surprising story of Merlin's lost years.

The story begins not with a wizard . . . but with a boy. A boy who is spat out by the sea and washes ashore on the rugged coast of Wales. Half-drowned, barely alive, he has no memory at all—no idea who he is. And much later, after many great adventures, the story ends with a young man, deeply wise, who is ready at last to step into a central place in Arthurian lore. And, as well, a central place in our hearts.

Sometimes I wonder whether that person who washed ashore on that fateful day was not just a boy, or a wizard, but something more. A metaphor, perhaps, for hidden gifts that each of us carries down inside—even when we feel most lost and alone. Whatever you conclude on that score, I hope that you will enjoy getting to know a whole new Merlin as much as I have.

So let us now gather round the wizard. Sit back, get comfortable. And listen well . . . as he reveals, at last, the secrets of his lost years.

T. A. BARRON

T. A. BARRON has led a diverse life, but it has always been marked by his love of family, the great outdoors, and writing. Throughout his youth—growing up on a ranch in Colorado, winning a Rhodes Scholarship to Oxford, and traveling widely with his backpack in Asia and Africa—those themes were paramount. During his years as president of a successful venture capital business, his own family grew, along with his passion for writing. Finally, in 1989, he surprised his business associates by resigning his management position, so that he could move back to Colorado and write books full time.

In Barron's words: "The world around us is full of wonder, mystery, and surprise. It gives us a chance to follow our dreams. And I love to explore it, whether by foot or by pen."

ᴛʜᴇ Lost Years
ᴏꜰ Merlin

Spat out by the sea, close to death, the boy lay on the sand. Even if he somehow survived, he had no home. No memory. And no name.

So begins the tale of the lone boy who washed ashore on a fateful day. Weak as he is, he vows to find his real home and his true name. He has no clue whatsoever that he will one day become Merlin, the legendary mage of Camelot who will be the greatest wizard of all time.

In search of the truth, he voyages to the mist-shrouded isle of Fincayra, an enchanted place "halfway between earth and heaven." There he makes three great friends: Rhia, a quirky and wise young woman who lives in the forest; Trouble, a feisty little hawk; and Shim, who stands only knee-high but is convinced that he's really a giant. And he makes one terrible enemy—the wicked warlord Rhita Gawr.

PROLOGUE

If I close my eyes, and breathe to the rolling rhythm of the sea, I can still remember that long ago day. Harsh, cold, and lifeless it was, as empty of promise as my lungs were empty of air.

Since that day, I have seen many others, more than I have the strength left to count. Yet that day glows as bright as the Galator itself, as bright as the day I found my own name, or the day I first cradled a baby who bore the name Arthur. Perhaps I remember it so clearly because the pain, like a scar on my soul, will not disappear. Or because it marked the ending of so much. Or, perhaps, because it marked a beginning as well as an ending: the beginning of my lost years.

A dark wave rose on the rolling sea, and from it lifted a hand.

As the wave surged higher, reaching toward sky as smoky gray as itself, the hand reached higher as well. A bracelet of foam swirled around the wrist, while desperate fingers groped for something they could not find. It was the hand of someone small. It was the hand of someone weak, too weak to fight any longer.

It was the hand of a boy.

With a deep sucking sound, the wave began to crest, tilting steadily toward the shore. For an instant it paused, hovering between ocean and land, between the brooding Atlantic and the perilous, rock-bound coast of Wales, known in those days as Gwynedd. Then the sucking swelled into a crashing roar as the wave toppled over, hurling the boy's limp body onto the black rocks.

His head smacked against a stone, so violently that his skull would surely have split open were it not for the thick mat of hair that covered it. He lay completely still, except when the whoosh of air from the next wave tousled his locks, black beneath the stains of blood.

A shabby seagull, seeing his motionless form, hopped over the jumble of rocks for a closer look. Bending its beak toward the boy's face, it tried to pull a strand of sea kelp that was wrapped around his ear. The bird tugged and twisted, squawking angrily.

At last the kelp broke free. Triumphantly, the bird jumped down to one of the boy's bare arms. Beneath the shreds of a brown tunic still clinging to him, he seemed small, even for a boy of seven years. Yet something about his face—the shape of his brow, perhaps, or the lines around his eyes—seemed far older.

At that instant, he coughed, vomited seawater, and

coughed again. With a screech, the gull dropped the kelp and fluttered off to a stony perch.

The boy remained motionless for a moment. All he could taste was sand, slime, and vomit. All he could feel was the painful throbbing of his head, and the rocks jabbing into his shoulders. Then came another cough, another gush of seawater. A halting, labored breath. Then a second breath, and a third. Slowly, his slender hand clenched into a fist.

Waves surged and subsided, surged and subsided. For a long while, the small candle flame of life in him wavered at the edge of darkness. Beneath the throbbing, his mind seemed strangely empty. Almost as if he had lost a piece of his very self. Or as if a kind of wall had been erected, cutting him off from a portion of himself, leaving nothing but a lingering sense of fear.

His breathing slowed. His fist relaxed. He gasped, as if to cough again, but instead fell still.

Cautiously, the seagull edged closer.

Then, from whatever quarter, a thin thread of energy began to move through his body. Something inside him was not yet ready to die. He stirred again, breathed again.

The gull froze.

He opened his eyes. Shivering with cold, he rolled to his side. Feeling the rough sand in his mouth, he tried to spit, but succeeded only in making himself gag from the rancid taste of kelp and brine.

With effort, he raised an arm and wiped his mouth with the tatters of his tunic. Then he winced, feeling the raw lump on the back of his head. Willing himself to sit up, he braced his elbow against a rock and pushed himself upright.

He sat there, listening to the grinding and splashing sea. Beyond the ceaseless pulsing of the waves, beyond the pounding inside his head, he thought for an instant that he could hear something else—a voice, perhaps. A voice from some other time, some other place, though he could not remember where.

With a sudden jolt, he realized that he could not remember *anything*. Where he had come from. His mother. His father. His name. *His own name*. Hard as he tried, he could not remember. *His own name*.

"Who am I?"

Hearing his cry, the gull squawked and took flight.

Catching sight of his reflection in a pool of water, he paused to look. A strange face, belonging to a boy he did not know, peered back at him. His eyes, like his hair, were as black as coal, with scattered flecks of gold. His ears, which were almost triangular and pointed at the top, seemed oddly large for the rest of his face. Likewise, his brow rose high above his eyes. Yet his nose looked narrow and slight, more a beak than a nose. Altogether, his face did not seem to belong to itself.

He mustered his strength and rose to his feet. Head swirling, he braced himself against a pinnacle of rock until the dizziness calmed.

His eyes roamed over the desolate coastline. Rocks upon rocks lay scattered everywhere, making a harsh black barrier to the sea. The rocks parted in only one place—and then only grudgingly—around the roots of an ancient oak tree. Its gray bark peeling, the old oak faced the ocean with the stance of centuries. There was a deep hollow in its trunk, gouged out by fire ages ago. Age warped its every branch, twisting some into knots. Yet it continued to stand, roots anchored, immutable against storm and sea. Behind the oak stood a dark grove of younger trees, and behind them, high cliffs loomed even darker.

Desperately, the boy searched the landscape for anything he might recognize, anything that might coax his memory to return. He recognized nothing.

He turned, despite the stinging salt spray, to the open sea. Waves rolled and toppled, one after another after another. Nothing but endless gray billows as far as he could see. He listened again for the mysterious voice, but heard only the distant call of a kittiwake perched on the cliffs.

Had he come from somewhere out there, beyond the sea?

Vigorously, he rubbed his bare arms to stop the shivers. Spying a loose clump of sea kelp on a rock, he picked it up. Once, he knew, this formless mass of green had danced with its own graceful rhythm, before being uprooted and cast adrift. Now it hung limp in his hand. He wondered why he himself had been uprooted, and from where.

A low, moaning sound caught his ear. That voice again! It came from the rocks beyond the old oak tree.

He lurched forward in the direction of the voice. For the first time he noticed a dull ache between his shoulder blades. He could only assume that his back, like his head, had slammed against the rocks. Yet the ache felt somehow deeper, as if something beneath his shoulders had been torn away long ago.

After several halting steps he made it to the ancient tree. He leaned against its massive trunk, his heart pounding. Again he heard the mysterious moaning. Again he set off.

Often his bare feet would slip on the wet rocks, pitching him sideways. Stumbling along, his torn brown tunic flapping about his legs, he resembled an ungainly water bird, picking his way across the shoreline. Yet all the time he knew what he really was: a lone boy, with no name and no home.

Then he saw her. Crumpled among the stones lay the body of a woman, her face beside a surging tidal pool. Her long, unbraided hair, the color of a yellow summer moon, spread about her head like rays of light. She had strong cheekbones and a complexion that would be described as creamy were it not tinged with blue. Her long blue robe, torn in places, was splotched with sand and sea kelp. Yet the quality of the wool, as well as the jeweled pendant on a leather cord around her neck, revealed her to have been once a woman of wealth and stature.

He rushed forward. The woman moaned again, a moan of inextinguishable pain. He could almost feel her agony, even as he could feel his own hopes rising. *Do I know her?* he asked himself as he bent over her twisted body. Then, from a place of deeper longing, *Does she know me?*

With a single finger he touched her cheek, as cold as the cold sea. He watched her take several short, labored breaths. He listened to her wretched moaning. And, with a sigh, he admitted to himself that she was, for him, a complete stranger.

Still, as he studied her, he could not suppress the hope that she might have arrived on this shore together with him. If she had not come on the same wave, then at least she might have come from the same place. Perhaps, if she lived, she might be able to fill the empty cup of his memory. Perhaps she knew his very name! Or the names of his mother and father. Or perhaps . . . she might actually *be* his mother.

A frigid wave slapped against his legs. His shivers returned, even as his hopes faded. She might not live, and even if she did, she probably would not know him. And she certainly could not be his mother. That was too much to hope for. Besides, she could not have looked less like him. She looked truly beautiful, even at the edge of death, as beautiful as an angel. And he had seen his own reflection. He knew what he looked like. Less like an angel than a bedraggled, half-grown demon.

A snarl erupted from behind his back.

The boy whirled around. His stomach clenched. There, in the shadows of the dark grove, stood an enormous wild boar.

A low, vicious growl vibrating in its throat, the boar stepped out of the trees. Bristling brown fur covered its entire body except for the eyes and a gray scar snaking down its left foreleg. Its tusks, sharp as daggers, were blackened with the blood of a previous kill. More frightening, though, were its red eyes, which glowed like hot coals.

The boar moved smoothly, almost lightly, despite its hulking form. The boy stepped backward. This beast outweighed him several times over. One kick of its leg would send him sprawling. One stab of its tusk would rip his flesh to shreds. Abruptly the boar stopped and hunched its muscular shoulders, preparing to charge.

Glancing behind, the boy could see only the onrushing waves of the ocean. No escape that way. He grabbed a crooked shard of driftwood to use as a weapon, though he knew it would not even begin to pierce the boar's hide. Even so, he tried to plant his feet on the slippery rocks, bracing for the attack.

Then he remembered. The hollow in the old oak! Although the tree stood about halfway between him and the boar, he might be able to get there first.

He started to dash for the tree, then suddenly caught himself. The woman. He could not just leave her there. Yet his own chance for safety depended on speed. Grimacing, he tossed aside the driftwood and grabbed her limp arms.

Straining his trembling legs, he tried to pull her free from the rocks. Whether from all the water she had swallowed or from the weight of death upon her, she felt as heavy as the rocks themselves. Finally, under the glaring eyes of the boar, she budged.

The boy began dragging her toward the tree. Sharp stones cut into his feet. Heart racing, head throbbing, he pulled with all his power.

The boar snarled again, this time more like a raspy laugh. The whole body of the beast tensed, nostrils flaring and tusks gleaming. Then it charged.

Though the boy was only a few feet from the tree, something kept him from running. He snatched a squarish stone from the ground and hurled it at the boar's head. Only an instant before reaching them, the boar changed direction. The stone whizzed past and clattered on the ground.

Amazed that he could have possibly daunted the beast, the boy quickly bent to retrieve another stone. Then, sensing some movement over his shoulder, he spun around.

Out of the bushes behind the ancient oak bounded an immense stag. Bronze in hue, except for the white boots on each leg that shone like purest quartz, the stag lowered its great rack of antlers. With the seven points on each side aimed like so many spears, the stag leaped at the boar. But the beast swerved aside just in time to dodge the thrust.

As the boar careened and snarled ferociously, the stag leaped once again. Seizing the moment, the boy dragged the limp woman into the hollow of the tree. By folding her legs tight against her chest, he pushed her entirely into the opening. The wood, still charred from some ancient fire, curled around her like a great black shell. He wedged himself into the small space beside her, as the boar and the stag circled each other, pawing the ground and snorting wrathfully.

Eyes aflame, the boar feigned a charge at the stag, then bolted straight at the tree. Hunched in the hollow, the boy drew back as far as he could. Yet his face remained so close to the gnarled bark of the opening that he still could feel the boar's hot breath as its tusks slashed wildly at the trunk. One of the tusks grazed the boy's face, gashing him just below the eye.

At that moment the stag plowed into the flank of the boar. The bulky beast flew into the air and landed on its side near the bushes. Blood oozing from a punctured thigh, the boar scrambled to its feet.

The stag lowered its head, poised to leap again. Hesitating for a split second, the boar snarled one final time before retreating into the trees.

With majestic slowness, the stag turned toward the boy. For a brief moment, their eyes met. Somehow the boy knew that he would remember nothing from that day so clearly as the bottomless brown pools of the stag's unblinking eyes, eyes as deep and mysterious as the ocean itself.

Then, as swiftly as it had appeared, the stag leaped over the twisted roots of the oak and vanished from sight.

1

A LİVİПG EYE

I stand alone, beneath the stars.

The entire sky ignites into flame, as if a new sun is being born. People shriek and scatter. But I stand there, unable to move, unable to breathe. Then I see the tree, darker than a shadow against the flaming sky. Its burning branches writhe like deadly serpents. They reach for me. The fiery branches come closer. I try to escape, but my legs are made of stone. My face is burning! I hide my eyes. I scream.

My face! My face is burning!

I awoke. Perspiration stung my eyes. Straw from my pallet scratched against my face.

Blinking, I drew a deep breath and wiped my face with my hands. They felt cool against my cheeks.

Stretching my arms, I felt again that pain between my shoulder blades. Still there! I wished it would go away.

Why should it still bother me now, more than five years since the day I had washed ashore? The wounds to my head had long since healed, though I still remembered nothing of my life before being thrown on the rocks. So why should this wound last so much longer? I shrugged. Like so much else, I would never know.

I started to stuff some loose straw back into the pallet when my fingers uncovered an ant, dragging the body of a worm several times its size. I watched, almost laughing, as the ant tried to climb straight up the miniature mountain of straw. It could have easily gone around one side or another. But no. Some mysterious motive drove it to try, spill over backward, try again, and spill again. For several minutes I watched this repeating performance.

At last I took pity on the little fellow. I reached for one of its legs, then realized that it might twist off, especially if the ant struggled. So I picked up the worm instead. Just as I expected, the ant clung to it, kicking frantically.

I carried the ant and its prize up and over the straw, dropping them gently on the other side. To my surprise, when I released my hold on the worm, so did the ant. It turned toward me, waving its tiny antennae wildly. I caught the distinct feeling that I was being scolded.

"My apologies," I whispered through my grin.

The ant scolded me for a few more seconds. Then it bit into the worm and started to drag the heavy load away. To its home.

My grin faded. Where could I find my own home? I would drag behind me this whole pallet, this whole hut if necessary, if only I knew where to go.

Turning to the open window above my head, I saw the full moon, glowing as bright as a pot of molten silver.

Moonlight poured through the window, and through the gaps in the thatched roof, painting the interior of the hut with its gleaming brush. For a moment, the moonlight nearly disguised the poverty of the room, covering the earthen floor with a sheath of silver, the rough clay walls with sparkles of light, the still-sleeping form in the corner with the glow of an angel.

Yet I knew that it was all an illusion, no more real than my dream. The floor was just dirt, the bed just straw, the dwelling just a hovel made of twigs bound with clay. The covered pen for the geese next door had been constructed with more care! I knew, for I sometimes hid myself in there, when the honking and hissing of geese sounded more to my liking than the howling and chattering of people. The pen stayed warmer than this hut in February, and drier in May. Even if I did not deserve any better than the geese, no one could doubt that Branwen did.

I watched her sleeping form. Her breathing, so subtle that it hardly lifted her woolen blanket, seemed calm and peaceful. Alas, I knew better. While peace might visit her in sleep, it escaped her in waking life.

She shifted in her slumber, rolling her face toward mine. In the lunar light she looked even more beautiful than usual, her creamy cheeks and brow thoroughly relaxed, as they were only on such nights when she slept soundly. Or in her moments of silent prayer, which happened more and more often.

I frowned at her. If only she would speak. Tell me what she knew. For if she did know anything about our past, she had refused to discuss it. Whether that was because she truly did not know, or because she simply did not want me to know, I could never tell.

And, in the five years we had shared this hut, she had revealed little more about herself. But for the kind touch of her hand and the ever-present sorrow at the back of her eyes, I hardly knew her at all. I only knew that she was not my mother, as she claimed.

How could I be so sure that she was not my mother? Somehow, in my heart, I knew. She was too distant, too secretive. Surely a mother, a real mother, wouldn't hide so much from her own son. And if I needed any more assurance, I had only to look at her face. So lovely—and so very different from my own. There was no hint of black in those eyes, nor of points on those ears! No, I was no more her son than the geese were my siblings.

Nor could I believe that her real name was Branwen, and that mine was Emrys, as she had tried to convince me. Whatever names we had possessed before the sea had spat us out on the rocks, I felt sure somehow that they were not those. As many times as she had called me Emrys, I could not shake the feeling that my true name was . . . something else. Yet I had no idea where to look for the truth, except perhaps in the wavering shadows of my dreams.

The only times that Branwen, if that was really her name, would show even a hint of her true self were when she told me stories. Especially the stories of the ancient Greeks. Those tales were clearly her favorites. And mine, too. Whether she knew it or not, some part of her seemed to come alive when she spoke of the giants and gods, the monsters and quests, in the Greek myths.

True, she also enjoyed telling tales of the Druid healers, or the miracle worker from Galilee. But her stories about the Greek gods and goddesses brought a special light into her sapphire eyes. At times, I almost felt that telling these stories was her way of talking about a place that she believed really existed—a place where strange creatures roamed the land and great spirits mingled with humans. The whole notion seemed foolish to me, but apparently not to her.

A sudden flash of light at her throat curtailed my thoughts. I knew that it was only the light of the moon reflected in her jeweled pendant, still hanging from the leather cord about her neck, although the green color seemed richer tonight than ever before. I realized that I had never seen her take the pendant off, not even for an instant.

Something tapped on the dirt behind me. I turned to see a bundle of dried leaves, slender and silvery in the moonlight, bound with a knot of grass. It must have fallen from the ridge beam above, which supported not only the thatch but also dozens of clusters of herbs, leaves, flowers, roots, nuts, bark shavings, and seeds. These were only a portion of Branwen's collection, for many more bundles hung from the window frame, the back of the door, and the tilting table beside her pallet.

Because of the bundles, the whole hut smelled of thyme, beech root, mustard seed, and more. I loved the aromas. Except for dill, which made me sneeze. Cedar bark, my favorite, lifted me as tall as a giant, petals of lavender tingled my toes, and sea kelp reminded me of something I could not quite remember.

All these ingredients and tools she used to make her healing powders, pastes, and poultices. Her table held a large assortment of bowls, knives, mortars, pestles, strainers, and other utensils. Often I watched her crushing

leaves, mixing powders, straining plants, or applying a
mixture of remedies to someone's wound or wart. Yet I
knew as little about her healing work as I did about her.
While she allowed me to watch, she would not converse
or tell stories. She merely worked away, usually singing
some chant or other.

Where had she learned so much about the art of healing? Where had she discovered the tales of so many distant lands and times? Where had she first encountered the
teachings of the man from Galilee that increasingly occupied her thoughts? She would not say.

I was not alone in being vexed by her silence. Often-
times the villagers would whisper behind her back, wondering about her healing powers, her unnatural beauty, her
strange chants. I had even heard the words *sorcery* and
black magic used once or twice, although it did not seem
to discourage people from coming to her when they
needed a boil healed, a cough cured, or a nightmare dis-
pelled.

Branwen herself did not seem worried by the whisper-
ings. As long as most people paid her for her help, so that
we could continue to make our way, she did not seem to
care what they might think or say. Recently she had
tended to an elderly monk who had slipped on the wet
stones of the mill bridge and gashed his arm. While binding his wound, Branwen uttered a Christian blessing,
which seemed to please him. When she followed it with
a Druid chant, however, he scolded her and warned her
against blasphemy. She replied calmly that Jesus himself
was so devoted to healing others that he might well have
drawn upon the wisdom of the Druids, as well as others
now called pagan. At that point the monk angrily shook

off her bandage and left, though not before telling half
the village that she was doing the work of demons.

I turned back to the pendant. It seemed to shine with
its own light, not just the moon's. For the first time I
noticed that the crystal in its center was not merely flat
green, as it appeared from a distance. Leaning closer, I
discovered violets and blues flowing like rivulets beneath
its surface, while glints of red pulsed with a thousand tiny
hearts. It looked almost like a living eye.

Galator. The word sprung suddenly into my mind. *It
is called Galator.*

I shook my head, puzzled. Where did that word come
from? I could not recall ever having heard it. I must have
picked it up from the village square, where numerous di-
alects—Celt, Saxon, Roman, Gaelic, and others even
more strange—collided and merged every day. Or perhaps
from one of Branwen's own stories, which were sprinkled
with words from the Greeks, the Jews, the Druids, and
others more ancient still.

"Emrys!"

Her shrill whisper startled me so much that I jumped.
I faced the bluer-than-blue eyes of the woman who shared
with me her hut and her meals, but nothing more.

"You are awake."

"I am. And you were staring at me strangely."

"Not at you," I replied. "At your pendant." On an im-
pulse, I added, "At your *Galator.*"

She gasped. With a sweep of her hand she stuffed the
pendant under her robe. Then, trying to keep her voice
calm, she said, "That is not a word I remember telling
you."

My eyes widened. "You mean it is the real word? The right word?"

She observed me thoughtfully, almost started to speak, then caught herself. "You should be sleeping, my son."

As always, I bristled when she called me that. "I can't sleep."

"Would a story help? I could finish the one about Apollo."

"No. Not now."

"I could make you a potion, then."

"No thanks." I shook my head. "When you did that for the thatcher's son, he slept for three and a half days."

A smile touched her lips. "He drank a week's dose at once, poor fool."

"It's almost dawn, anyway."

She gathered her rough wool blanket. "Well, if you don't want to sleep, I do."

"Before you do, can't you tell me more about that word? Gal—Oh, what was it?"

Seeming not to hear me, she wrapped herself in her customary cloak of silence, even as she wrapped herself in the wool blanket and closed her eyes once more. In seconds, she seemed to be asleep again. Yet the peace I had seen in her face before had flown.

"Can't you tell me?"

She did not stir.

"Why don't you ever help me?" I wailed. "I need your help!"

Still she did not stir.

Ruefully, I watched her for a while. Then I rolled off the pallet, stood, and splashed my face with water from the large wooden bowl by the door. Glancing again at

Branwen, I felt a renewed surge of anger. Why wouldn't she answer me? Why wouldn't she help me? Yet even as I looked upon her, I felt a small prick of guilt that I had never been able to bring myself to call her Mother, although I knew how much it would please her. And yet . . . what kind of mother would refuse to help her son?

I tugged against the rope handle of the door. With a scrape against the dirt, it opened, and I left the hut.

THE SEVEN SONGS OF MERLIN

Young Merlin's nemesis, the wicked Rhita Gawr, is back—and more determined than ever to conquer the enchanted isle of Fincayra. But first he must get rid of Merlin, whose powers continue to grow. Rhita Gawr plots to attack Merlin just at the moment when the young man finally reunites with his beloved mother. The attack, though, goes awry and strikes Merlin's mother instead.

There is only one way to save her. Merlin must solve an ancient riddle known as the Seven Songs of Wisdom. And he must do it in just a few short days.

PROLOGUE

How the centuries have flown . . . Faster, by far, than the brave hawk who once bore me on his back. Faster, indeed, than the arrow of pain that lodged in my heart on the day I lost my mother.

Still I can see the Great Council of Fincayra, gathering in the circle of standing stones, all that remained of the mighty castle after the Dance of the Giants. Not for many ages had a Great Council been called on that spot; not for many ages would one be called again. Several difficult questions awaited resolution by the delegates, including how to punish the fallen monarch, and whether or not to choose a successor. But the gravest question of all was what to do with the enchanted Treasures of Fincayra, especially the Flowering Harp.

I cannot forget how the meeting began. Nor, hard as I try, can I forget how it ended.

•   •   •

A cluster of shadows more dark than the night, the circle
of stones stood erect on the ridge.

No stirring, no sound, disturbed the night air. A lone
bat swooped toward the ruins, then veered away, perhaps
out of fear that the Shrouded Castle might somehow rise
again. But all that remained of its towers and battlements
was the ring of standing stones, as silent as abandoned
graves.

Slowly, a strange light began rippling over the stones.
It was not the light of the sun, still hours from rising, but
of the stars overhead. Bit by bit the stars grew steadily
brighter. It seemed as if they were somehow drawing
nearer, pressing closer to the circle, watching with a thousand eyes aflame.

A broad-winged moth, as yellow as butter, alighted on
one of the stones. Soon it was joined by a pale blue bird,
and an ancient horned owl missing many feathers. Something slithered across a fallen pillar, keeping to the shadows. A pair of fauns, with the legs and hoofs of goats and
the chests and faces of boys, gamboled into the clearing
inside the circle. Next came the walking trees, ashes and
oaks and hawthorns and pines, sweeping across the ridge
like a dark green tide.

Seven Fincayran men and women, their eyes full of
wonder, stepped into the circle alongside a band of red-
bearded dwarves, a black stallion, several ravens, a pair
of water nymphs raucously splashing each other in a pool
beneath one of the stones, a speckled lizard, popinjays,
peacocks, a unicorn whose coat shone as white as her
horn, a family of green beetles who had brought their own
leaf to sit on, a doe with her fawn, a huge snail, and a

phoenix who stared at the crowd continuously without ever blinking.

As more delegates arrived, one of the Fincayrans, a shaggy-headed poet with a tall brow and dark, observant eyes, stood watching the scene unfold. In time, he stepped over to a tumbled pillar and sat down next to a robust girl dressed in a suit of woven vines. On her other side sat a boy, holding a twisted staff, who looked older than his thirteen years. His eyes, blacker than charcoal, seemed strangely distant. He had recently taken to calling himself Merlin.

Screeching and fluttering, buzzing and growling, hissing and bellowing filled the air. As the sun rose higher, painting the circle of stones with golden hues, the din rose higher as well. The cacophonous noise subsided only once, when an enormous white spider, more than twice as big as the stallion, entered the ring. As the other creatures hushed, they moved quickly aside, for while they might have felt honored to be joined by the legendary Grand Elusa, they also suspected that she might well have worked up an appetite on her journey from her crystal cave in the Misted Hills. She had no difficulty finding a seat.

As the Grand Elusa positioned herself on a heap of crushed rock, she scratched the hump on her back with one of her eight legs. Using another leg, she pulled a large, brown sack off her back and placed it by her side. Then she glanced around the circle, pausing for an instant to gaze at Merlin.

Still more came. A centaur, wearing a beard that fell almost down to his hooves, strode solemnly into the ring. A pair of foxes, tails held high, pranced in his wake, followed by a young wood elf with arms and legs nearly as wispy as her nut brown hair. A living stone, splotched with moss, rolled into the center, barely missing a slow-moving hedgehog. A swarm of energetic bees hovered close to the ground. Near the edge, a family of ogres viciously scratched and bit each other to pass the time.

And still more came, many Merlin could not identify. Some looked like bristling bushes with fiery eyes, others resembled twisted sticks or clumps of mud, and still others seemed invisible but for a vague shimmer of light they cast on the stones. He saw creatures with bizarre faces, dangerous faces, curious faces, or no faces at all. In less than an hour, the silent ring of stones had transformed into something more like a carnival.

The poet, Cairpré, did his best to answer Merlin's questions about the strange and wondrous creatures surrounding them. That, he explained, was a snow hen, who remained as elusive as a moonbeam. And that, a glynmater, who ate food only once every six hundred years—and then only the leaves of the tendradil flower. Some creatures he could not recognize were known by the leaf-draped girl, Rhia, from her years in Druma Wood. Yet there remained several that neither Cairpré nor Rhia could identify.

That came as no surprise. No one alive, except possibly . . . the Grand Elusa, had ever seen all of the diverse residents of Fincayra. Soon after the Dance of the Giants had occurred, toppling the wicked king Stangmar and destroying his Shrouded Castle, the call had risen from many quarters to convene a Great Council. For the first time in living memory, all the mortal citizens of Fincayra, whether bird or beast or insect or something else entirely, were invited to send representatives to an assembly.

Almost every race had responded. The few missing ones included the warrior goblins and shifting wraiths, who had been driven back into the caves of the Dark Hills after the defeat of Stangmar; the treelings, who had disappeared from the land long ago; and the mer people, who inhabited the waters surrounding Fincayra but could not be found in time to be invited.

After studying the crowd, Cairpré observed sadly that the great canyon eagles, one of the oldest races on Fincayra, were also not present. In ancient times the stirring cry of a canyon eagle always marked the beginning of a Great Council. Not this time, however, since the forces of Stangmar had hunted the proud birds to extinction. That cry, Cairpré concluded, would never again echo among the hills of this land.

Merlin then glimpsed a pale, bulbous hag with no hair on her head and no mercy in her eyes. He shivered with recognition. Although she had taken many names across the ages, she was most often called Domnu, meaning Dark Fate. No sooner had he caught sight of her than she vanished into the throng. He knew she was avoiding him. He also knew why.

Suddenly a great rumbling, even louder than the noise of the assembly, shook the ridge. One of the standing stones wobbled precariously. The rumbling grew still louder, causing the stone to crash to the ground, almost crushing the doe and fawn. Merlin and Rhia looked at each other—not with fright, but with understanding. For they had heard the footsteps of giants before.

Two gargantuan figures, each as tall as the castle that had once stood on this spot, strode up to the circle. From far away in the mountains they had come, leaving the rebuilding of their ancestral city of Varigal long enough to join the Great Council. Merlin turned, hoping to find his friend Shim. But Shim was not among the new arrivals. The boy sighed, telling himself that Shim would probably have slept through the meeting anyway.

The first giant, a wild-haired female with bright green eyes and a crooked mouth, grunted and bent down to pick up the fallen stone. Although twenty horses would have strained to move it, she placed it back in position without any difficulty. Meanwhile, her companion, a ruddy-skinned fellow with arms as thick as oak trunks, placed his hands on his hips and surveyed the scene. After a long moment, he gave her a nod.

She nodded in return. Then, with another grunt, she lifted both of her hands into the air, seeming to grasp at the streaming clouds. Seeing this, Cairpré raised his bushy eyebrows in puzzlement.

High in the sky, a tiny black dot appeared. Out of the clouds it spiraled, as if caught in an invisible whirlpool. Lower and lower it came, until every eye of every creature in the circle was trained on it. A new hush blanketed the assembly. Even the irrepressible water nymphs fell silent.

The dot grew larger as it descended. Soon massive wings could be seen, then a broad tail, then sunlight glinting on a hooked beak. A sudden screech ripped the air, echoing from one ridge to another, until the land itself seemed to be answering the call. The call of a canyon eagle.

The powerful wings spread wide, stretching out like a sail. Then the wings angled backward, as enormous talons thrust toward the ground. Rabbits and foxes squealed at the sight, and many more beasts cringed. With a single majestic flap, the great canyon eagle settled on the shoulder of the wild-haired giant.

The Great Council of Fincayra had begun.

As the first order of business, the delegates agreed that no one should leave the meeting until all the questions had been decided. Also, at the request of the mice, each of the delegates promised not to eat anyone else during the course of the proceedings. Only the foxes objected to this idea, arguing that the question of what to do with the Flowering Harp alone could take several days to resolve. Even so, the rule was adopted. To ensure compliance, the Grand Elusa herself kindly offered to enforce it. Though she never said just how she planned to do that, no one seemed inclined to ask her.

As its next act, the assembly declared the circle of stones itself a sacred monument. Clearing her throat with the subtlety of a rockslide, the wild-haired giant proposed that the ruins of the Shrouded Castle receive a new name: Dance of the Giants, or *Estonahenj* in the giants' own ancient tongue. The assembled delegates adopted the name unanimously, though a heavy silence fell over the circle. For while the Dance of the Giants signified Fincayra's hope for a brighter future, it was the kind of hope that springs only from the most profound sorrow.

In time, the discussion turned to the fate of Stangmar. While the wicked king had been overthrown, his life had been saved—by none other than Merlin, his only son. Although Merlin himself, being only part Fincayran, was not allowed to voice his own views at the assembly, the poet Cairpré offered to speak on his behalf. After hearing the boy's plea that his father's life, no matter how wretched, should be spared, the Great Council argued for hours. Finally, over the strong objections of the giants and the canyon eagle, the assembly decided that Stangmar should be imprisoned for the rest of his days in one of the inescapable caverns north of the Dark Hills.

Next came the question of who should rule Fincayra. The bees suggested that their own queen could rule everyone, but that notion found no support. So fresh was the agony of Stangmar's kingship that many delegates spoke passionately against having any leader at all. Not even a parliament of citizens would do, they argued, for in time power always corrupts. Cairpré, for his part, denounced such thinking as folly. He cited examples of anarchy that had brought ruin to other peoples, and warned that without any leadership at all Fincayra would again fall prey to that nefarious warlord of the Otherworld, Rhita Gawr. Yet most of the delegates dismissed his concerns. The Great Council voted overwhelmingly to do without any leadership whatsoever.

Then came the gravest question of all. What should be done with the Treasures of Fincayra?

As everyone watched in awe, the Grand Elusa opened the sack by her side and removed the Flowering Harp. Its oaken sound box, inlaid with ash and carved with floral designs, gleamed eerily. A green butterfly wafted over and alighted on its smallest string. With the swipe of one enormous leg, the Grand Elusa shooed the butterfly away, causing the string to tinkle gently. After pausing to listen, she then removed the rest of the Treasures: the sword Deepercut, the Caller of Dreams, the Orb of Fire, and six of the Seven Wise Tools (the seventh one, alas, had been lost in the collapse of the castle).

All eyes examined the Treasures. For a long interval, no one stirred. The stones themselves seemed to lean forward to get a closer look. The delegates knew that, long before the rise of Stangmar, these fabled Treasures had belonged to all Fincayrans, and were shared freely throughout the land. Yet that had left the Treasures vulnerable to thievery, as Stangmar had demonstrated. A spotted hare suggested that each Treasure ought to have a guardian, someone responsible for guarding it and seeing that it was used wisely. That way the Treasures could be shared, but still protected. Most of the representatives agreed. They urged the Grand Elusa to choose the guardians.

The great spider, however, declined. She declared that only someone much wiser could make such important selections. It would take a true wizard—someone like Tuatha, whose knowledge had been so vast, it was said, that he had even found a secret pathway to the Otherworld to consult with Dagda, greatest of all the spirits. But Tuatha had died years ago. In the end, after much urging, the Grand Elusa agreed to watch over the Treasures in her crystal cave, but only until the right guardians could be found.

While that solved the problem of the Treasures for the time being, it did not answer the question of the Flowering Harp. The surrounding countryside, afflicted by the Blight of Rhita Gawr, showed no sign of life, not even a sprig of green grass. The Dark Hills, especially, needed help, for the damage there had been the most severe. Only the magic of the Harp could revive the land.

Yet who should be the one to carry it? The Harp had not been played for many years, since Tuatha himself had used it to heal the forest destroyed by the dragon of the Lost Lands. While that forest had eventually returned to life, Tuatha had admitted that playing the Harp had required even more of his skill than lulling the enraged dragon into enchanted sleep. The Harp, he had warned, would only respond to the touch of someone with the heart of a wizard.

The oldest of the peacocks was the first to try. Spreading his radiant tail feathers to the widest, he strutted over to the Harp and lowered his head. With a swift stroke of his beak, he plucked one of the strings. A pure, resonant tone poured forth, lingering in the air. But nothing else happened. The Harp's magic lay dormant. Again the peacock tried, again with no result beyond a single note.

One by one, several other delegates came forward. The unicorn, her white coat glistening, slid her horn across the strings. A stirring chord resulted, but nothing more. Then came an immense brown bear, a dwarf whose beard fell below his knees, a sturdy-looking woman, and one of the water nymphs, all without success.

At last, a tan-colored toad hopped out of the shadows by Merlin's feet and over to the Grand Elusa. Stopping just beyond the great spider's reach, the toad rasped, "You may not be a wizarrrrd yourrrrself, but I rrrreally believe you have the hearrrrt of one. Would you carrrry the Harrrrp?"

The Grand Elusa merely shook her head. Lifting three of her legs, she pointed in the direction of Cairpré.

"Me?" sputtered the poet. "You can't be serious! I have no more the heart of a wizard than the head of a pig. *My knowledge so spare, my wisdom too rare.* I could never make the Harp respond." Stroking his chin, he turned to the boy by his side. "But I can think of someone else who might."

"The boy?" growled the brown bear skeptically, even as the boy himself shifted with unease.

"I don't know whether he has the heart of a wizard," Cairpré acknowledged, with a sidelong glance at Merlin. "I doubt even he knows."

The bear slammed his paw against the ground. "Then why do you propose him?"

The poet almost smiled. "Because I think there is more to him than meets the eye. He did, after all, destroy the Shrouded Castle. Let him try his hand with the Harp."

"I agree," declared a slender owl with a snap of her jaws. "He is the grandson of Tuatha."

"And the son of Stangmar," roared the bear. "Even if he can awaken its magic, he cannot be trusted."

Into the center of the circle stepped the wood elf, her nut brown hair rippling like a stream. She bowed slightly to Rhia, who returned the gesture. Then, in a lilting voice, she addressed the group. "The boy's father I know not, though I am told that, in his youth, he often played in Druma Wood. And, like the twisted tree that might have grown straight and tall, I cannot say whether the fault lay with him or with the elders who did not give him their support. Yet I did know the boy's mother. We called her Elen of the Sapphire Eyes. She healed me once, when I was aflame with fever. There was magic in her touch, more magic than even she understood. Perhaps her son has the same gift. I say we should let him try the Harp."

A wave of a agreement flowed through the assembly. The bear paced back and forth, grumbling to himself, but finally did not object.

As Merlin rose from the pillar, Rhia wrapped her leaf-draped arm around his own. He glanced at her gratefully, then stepped slowly over to the Harp. As he carefully retrieved it, cradling the sound box in his arms, the assembled delegates fell silent once again. The boy drew a deep breath, raised his hand, and plucked one of the strings. A deep note hung in the air, vibrating, for a long moment.

Sensing nothing remarkable had happened, Merlin turned a disappointed face toward Rhia and Cairpré. The brown bear growled in satisfaction. All at once, the canyon eagle, still perched on the giant's shoulder, screeched. Others joined the cry, roaring and howling and thumping with enthusiasm. For there, curling over the toe of Merlin's own boot, was a single blade of grass, as green as a rainwashed sapling. He smiled and plucked the string again, causing several more blades of grass to spring forth.

When, at last, the commotion subsided, Cairpré strode over to Merlin and clasped his hand. "Well done, my boy, well done." Then he paused. "It is a grave responsibility, you know, healing the lands."

Merlin swallowed. "I know."

"Once you begin this task, you must not rest until it is finished. Even now, the forces of Rhita Gawr are making plans for a renewed assault. You may be certain of that! The Dark Hills, where many of the forces lie hidden in caves and crevasses, are the lands most scarred from Blight—and also most vulnerable to attack. Our best protection is to restore the hills quickly so that peaceful creatures may return there to live. That will discourage the invaders, and also ensure that the rest of Fincayra will have warning of any attack."

He tapped the oaken instrument gently. "So you must begin in the Dark Hills—and remain there until the job is done. Save the Rusted Plains, and the other lands yearning to live again, until later. The Dark Hills must be healed before Rhita Gawr returns, or we will have lost our only chance."

He chewed his lip thoughtfully. "And one thing more, my boy. Rhita Gawr, when he does return, will be looking for you. To show his gratitude for how much trouble you have caused him. So avoid doing anything that might attract his attention. Just stick to your work, healing the Dark Hills."

"But what if, after I've left here, I can't make the Harp work?"

"If the Harp simply does not respond to your touch, we will understand. But remember: If you can make it work but shirk your task, you will never be forgiven."

Merlin nodded slowly. As the delegates looked on, he started to slip the Harp's leather sling over his shoulder.

"Wait!"

It was the voice of the hag, Domnu. Advancing toward the boy, she opened wide her eyes, sending waves of wrinkles across the top of her scalp. Then she lifted her arm and pointed a knobby finger at him. "The half-human boy cannot carry the Harp. He must leave this island! For if he stays, Fincayra is doomed."

Nearly everyone cringed at her words, none more than Merlin himself. They carried strange power, cutting deeper than any sword.

Domnu shook her finger. "If he does not leave, and

soon, all of us will perish." A chill wind passed through the circle, making even the giants shiver. "Have you all forgotten the prohibition, laid down by Dagda himself, against anyone with human blood remaining long on this island? Have you all forgotten that this boy was also born here, despite an even more ancient prohibition? If you let him carry the Harp, he will surely claim Fincayra as his rightful home. He probably has no intention of returning to the world beyond the mist. Heed my warning. This boy could upset the very balance between the worlds! He could bring the wrath of Dagda down upon us all. Even worse," she added with a leer, "he could be a tool of Rhita Gawr, like his father before him."

"I am not!" Merlin objected. "You just want me banished so you don't have to give me back the Galator."

Domnu's eyes flamed. "There, you see? He is speaking to the Great Council, even though he is not truly one of us. He has no respect for Fincayra's laws, just as he has no respect for the truth. The sooner he is exiled, the better."

Many heads nodded in the crowd, caught by the spell of her words. Merlin started to speak again, but someone else spoke first.

It was Rhia. Her gray-blue eyes alight, she faced the hairless hag. "I don't believe you. I just don't." Drawing a deep breath, she added, "And aren't you the one who has forgotten something? That prophecy, that very old prophecy, that only a child of human blood can defeat Rhita Gawr and those who serve him! What if that means Merlin? Would you still want us to send him away?"

Domnu opened her mouth, baring her blackened teeth, then shut it tight.

"The giiirl speeeaks the truuuth," thundered the deep voice of the Grand Elusa. Lifting her vast bulk with her eight legs, she peered straight at Domnu. "The boooy shooould staaay."

As if the spell had been broken, delegates of all descriptions thumped, growled, or flapped their agreement. Seeing this, Domnu grimaced. "I warned you," the hag grumbled. "That boy will be the ruin of us all."

Cairpré shook his head. "Time will tell."

Domnu glared at him. Then she turned and disappeared into the crowd—but not before shooting a glance at Merlin that made his stomach clench.

Rhia turned to Cairpré. "Aren't you going to help him put it on?"

The poet laughed, tossing his shaggy mane. "Of course." He lifted the Harp's leather sling over Merlin's head, resting it on the boy's shoulder. "You know this is a responsibility, my boy. All of us depend on you. Even so, may it also be a joy! With every strum of those strings, may you bring another field to flower."

He paused, gazing thoughtfully at Merlin. Lowering his voice, he added, "And may you heal yourself, even as you heal the land."

A roar of approval echoed around the sacred ring. With that, the Great Council of Fincayra disbanded.

THE FIRES OF MERLIN

Wings of Fire, the legendary dragon who has been asleep for a thousand years, has awakened in a fury. His last surviving children have been destroyed, and he blames young Merlin for this terrible deed. Enraged, the enormous dragon sets out to destroy the whole isle of Fincayra—and Merlin as well.

Before he can face the dragon's fiery breath, Merlin must confront some other kinds of fires. He descends into the heart of a volcano, fights the dreaded kreelixes who devour magic, and outwits the powerful queen Urnalda. And he finds the first fires of passion inside himself: for Hallia, a beautiful young woman with many secrets.

PROLOGUE

The mists of memory gather, the more with each passing year. Yet one day remains as clear in my mind as this morning's sunrise, although it happened those many centuries ago.

It was a day darkened by mists of its own, and by smoke thick and wrathful. While the fate of all Fincayra hung in the balance, no mortal creature suspected. For the mists of that day obscured everything but the fear, and the pain, and only the slightest hint of hope.

As still as a mountain for years beyond count, the massive gray boulder quite suddenly stirred.

It was not the fast-flowing water of the River Unceasing, slapping against the base of the boulder, that caused the change. Nor was it the sleek otter whose favorite pastime had long been sliding down the cleft between the boulder and the river's muddy bank. Nor the family of speckled lizards who had lived for generations in the patch of moss on the boulder's north side.

No, the stirring of the boulder on that day came from an entirely different source. One that, unlike the lizards, had never been seen at the spot, although it had in fact been present long before the first lizard ever arrived. For the source of the stirring came from deep within the boulder itself.

As mist gathered within the banks of the river, resting on the water like a thick white cloak, a faint scraping sound filled the air. A moment later, the boulder wobbled ever so slightly. With shreds of mist curling about its base, it suddenly pitched to one side. Hissing with alarm, three lizards leaped off and scurried away.

If the lizards had hoped to find a new home in the moss atop one of the other boulders, they were destined to be disappointed. For more scraping sounds joined with the constant splashing of the current. One by one, each of the nine boulders lining the river began to wobble, then rock vigorously, as if shaken by a tremor that only they could feel. One of them, partly submerged by the rushing river, started rolling toward a grove of hemlocks on the bank.

Near the top of the first boulder to come to life, a tiny crack appeared. Another crack split off, and then another. All at once, a jagged chip broke away, leaving a hole that glowed with a strange orange light. Slowly, tentatively, something started pushing its way out of the hole. It glistened darkly, even as it scraped against the surface.

It was a claw.

•   •   •

Far to the north, in the desolate ridges of the Lost Lands, a trail of smoke rose skyward, curling like a venomous snake. Nothing else moved on these slopes, not even an insect or a blade of grass trembling in the wind. These lands had been scorched by fire—so powerful that it had obliterated trees, evaporated rivers, and demolished even rocks, leaving behind nothing but charred ridges coated with ash. For these lands had long been the lair of a dragon.

Ages before, at the height of his wrath, the dragon had incinerated whole forests and swallowed entire villages. Valdearg—whose name, in Fincayra's oldest tongue, meant *Wings of Fire*—was the last and most feared of a long line of emperor dragons. Much of Fincayra had been blackened by his fiery breath, and all its inhabitants lived in terror of his shadow. Finally, the powerful wizard Tuatha had managed to drive the dragon back to his lair. After a prolonged battle, Valdearg had at last succumbed to the wizard's enchantment of sleep. He had remained in his flame-seared hollow, slumbering fitfully, ever since.

While many Fincayrans grumbled that Tuatha should have killed the dragon when he had the chance, others argued that the wizard must have spared him for a reason—though what that reason could possibly be no one knew. At least, in slumber, Wings of Fire could cause no more harm. Time passed, so much time that many people began to doubt that he would ever wake again. Some even questioned the old stories of his rampages. Others went further, wondering whether he had ever really existed, although very few indeed were willing to travel all the way to the Lost Lands to find out. Of those who did set out on the dangerous trek, very few ever returned.

Very little of what Tuatha had said at the conclusion of the Battle of Bright Flames had been understandable, for he spoke in riddles. And many of his words had been long forgotten. Still, a few bards kept alive what remained in the form of a poem called *The Dragon's Eye*. Although the poem had many versions, each as obscure as the others, all agreed that on some dark day in the future, Valdearg would awaken once more.

Even now, these lands reeked of charcoal. Near the hollow, the air shimmered with the unremitting heat of the dragon's breath. The low, roaring sound of his snoring echoed across the blackened ridges, while the dark column of smoke continued to pour from his nostrils, lifting slowly skyward.

The claw pushed higher, tapping the edge of the rock-like shell as cautiously as someone about to step on a frozen pond would tap the ice. Finally, the dagger-sharp tip of the claw dug into the surface, shooting cracks in all directions. A muffled sound, part screech and part grunt, came from deep inside. Then, all at once, the claw ripped away a large section of shell.

The enormous egg rocked again, rolling farther down the riverbank. As it splashed in the surging water, several more pieces of the shell dropped away. Although the morning sun had started to burn through the mist, its light did not diminish the orange glow radiating from the gaping hole.

More cracks snaked around the sides. The claw, curved like a huge hook, slashed at the edges of the hole, spraying fragments of shell in the river and on the muddy bank. With another grunt, the creature inside shoved the claw completely out of the hole, revealing a twisted, gangly arm covered with iridescent purple scales. Next came a hunched, bony shoulder, dripping with lavender-colored ooze. Hanging limp from the shoulder was a crumpled fold of leathery skin that might have been a wing.

Then, for whatever reason, the arm and shoulder fell still. For a long moment the egg neither rocked nor emitted any sound.

Suddenly the entire top half of the egg flew off, landing with a splash in the shallows. Rays of orange light shot into the shredding mist. Awkwardly, hesitantly, the scaly shoulder lifted, supporting a thin, purple neck flecked with scarlet spots. Hanging heavily from the neck, a head— twice as big as that of a full-grown horse—slowly lifted into the air. Above the massive jaw, studded with row upon row of gleaming teeth, a pair of immense nostrils twitched, sniffing the air for the first time.

From the creature's two triangular eyes, the orange light poured like glowing lava. The eyes, blinking every few seconds, gazed through the mist at the other eggs that had also begun to crack open. Raising one of her claws, the creature tried to scratch the bright yellow bump that protruded from the middle of her forehead. But her aim was off and instead she poked the soft, crinkled skin of her nose.

With a loud whimper, she shook her head vigorously, flapping her blue, banner-like ears against her head. After the shaking ceased, however, her right ear refused to lie flat again. Unlike the left one, which hung almost down to her shoulder, it stretched out to the side like a misplaced horn. Only the gentle droop at the tip hinted that it was, in fact, an ear.

• • •

Deep within the smoking cavern, the gargantuan form shifted uneasily. Valdearg's head, nearly as broad as a hill, jerked suddenly, crushing a pile of skulls long ago blackened by flames. His breath came faster and faster, roaring like a thousand waterfalls. Although his enormous eyes remained closed, his claws slashed ruthlessly at some invisible foe.

The dragon's tail lashed out, smashing against the charred wall of stone. He growled, less at the rocks that tumbled onto the green and orange scales of his back than at the torments of his dream—a dream that pushed him to the very edge of awakening. One of his vast wings batted the air. As the wing's edge scraped the floor of the hollow, dozens of jeweled swords and harnesses, gilded harps and trumpets, and polished gems and pearls flew in every direction. Clouds of smoke darkened the day.

The creature in the egg, her nose still throbbing, flashed her eyes angrily. Feeling an ancient urge, she drew a deep breath of air, puffing out her purple chest. With a sudden snort, she exhaled, flaring her nostrils. But no flames came, nor even a thin trail of smoke. For although she was, indeed, a baby dragon, she could not yet breathe fire.

Crestfallen, the baby dragon whimpered again. She lifted one leg to climb the rest of the way out of the shell, then halted abruptly. Hearing something, she cocked her head to one side. With one ear dangling like a thin blue flag and the other soaring skyward, she listened intently, not daring to move.

Suddenly the hatchling drew back in fright, teetering in the remains of the egg. For she had only just noticed the dark shadow forming in the mist on the far bank of the river. Sensing danger, she huddled deeper in the shell. Yet she could not keep her one unruly ear from poking over the rim.

After a long moment, she raised her head ever so slightly. Her heart thumped within her chest. She watched the shadow draw slowly nearer, wading through the churning water. As it approached, it started to harden into a strange, two-legged figure—carrying a curved blade that gleamed ominously. Then, with a start, she realized that the blade was lifting to strike.

1

THE LAST STRING

"Just one more."

Even as I spoke the words, I could scarcely believe them. I slid my hand across the scaly, gray-brown bark of the rowan tree whose massive roots encircled me, feeling the gentle slopes and curves of the living wood. In one hollow, as deep as a large bowl, sat some of the tools I had been using over the past several months: a stone hammer, a wedge of iron, three filing rods of different textures, and a carving knife no bigger than my little finger. I reached past them, past the knobbed root that served as a hanging rack for my larger saws, to the thin shelf of bark that had so recently held all eight strings.

Eight strings. Each one cured, stretched, and finally serenaded under the full autumn moon, according to ancient tradition. Thankfully, my mentor, Cairpré, had devoted weeks before that night to helping me learn all the intricate verses and melodies. Even so, the moon had nearly set before I finally sang every one of them correctly—and in the right order. Now seven of the strings gleamed on the little instrument propped on the root before me.

Grasping the last remaining string, the smallest of the lot, I brought it closer. As I twirled it slowly, its ends twisted and swayed—alive, almost. Like the tongue of someone on the very verge of speaking.

Late afternoon light played on the string, making it shine as golden as the autumn leaves speckling the grass at the base of the rowan tree. It felt surprisingly heavy, given its short length, yet as flexible as the breeze itself. Gently, I draped it on a cluster of dark red berries hanging from one of the rowan's lower boughs. Turning back to the instrument, I inserted the last two knobs, carved from the same branch of hawthorn as the others, whose month-long kiln drying had ended only yesterday. Rubbing against the oaken soundboard, the knobs squeaked ever so slightly.

At last, I retrieved the string. After tying the seven loops of a wizard's knot on each of the two knobs, I began twisting, one to the right and the other to the left. Gradually, the string tightened, straightening out like a wind-blown banner. Before it had grown too tight, I stopped. Now all that remained was to insert the bridge—and play.

Leaning back against the trunk of the rowan, I gazed at my handiwork. It was a psaltery, shaped something like a tiny harp but with a bowed soundboard behind all the strings. I lifted it off the root, studying it admiringly. Though it was barely as big as my open hand, it seemed to me as grand as a newborn star.

My own instrument. Made with my own hands.

I ran my finger along the strip of ash inlaid at the top of the frame. This would be much more than a source of music, I knew. Unless, of course, I had bungled any of the steps in making it. Or, much worse, unless . . .

I drew a slow, unsteady breath. Unless I lacked the one thing Cairpré couldn't teach me, the one thing he couldn't even describe—what he could only call *the essential core of a wizard*. For, as he had so often reminded me, the making of a wizard's first instrument was a sacred tradition, marking a gifted youth's coming of age. If the process succeeded, when the time finally came to play the instrument, it would release its own music. And, simultaneously, an entirely new level of the youth's own magic.

And if the process did not succeed . . .

I set down the psaltery. The strings jangled softly as the sound-board again touched the burly roots of the tree. Among these very roots, Fincayra's most famous wielders of magic—including my legendary grandfather, Tuatha—had cobbled their own first instruments. Hence the tree's name, written into many a ballad and tale: the Cobblers' Rowan.

Placing my hand over a rounded knob of bark, I listened for the pulse of life within the great tree. The slow, swelling rhythm of roots plunging deeper and branches reaching higher, of thousands of leaves melting from green to gold, of the tree itself breathing. Inhaling life, and death, and the mysterious bonds connecting both. The Cobblers' Rowan had continued to stand through many storms, many centuries—and many wizards. Did it know even now, I wondered, whether my psaltery would really work?

Lifting my gaze, I surveyed the hills of Druma Wood,

each one as round as the back of a running deer. Autumn hues shone scarlet, orange, yellow, and brown. Brightly plumed birds lifted out of the branches, chattering and cooing, while spirals of mist rose from hidden swamps. I could hear, weaving with the breeze, the continuous tumble of a waterfall. This forest, wilder than any place I had ever known, was truly the heart of Fincayra. It was the first place I had wandered after washing ashore on the island—and the first place I had ever felt my own roots sinking deeply.

I smiled, seeing my staff leaning against the rowan's trunk. That, too, had been a gift of this forest, as its spicy scent of hemlock reminded me constantly. Whatever elements of real magic that I possessed—outside of a few simple skills such as my second sight, which had come to me after I lost the use of my eyes, and my sword with some magic of its own—resided within the gnarled wood of that staff.

As did so much more. For my staff had, somehow, been touched by the power of Tuatha himself. He had reached out of the ages, out of the grave, to place his own magic within its shaft. Even with the blurred edges of my vision, I could make out the symbols carved upon it, symbols of the powers that I yearned to master fully: Leaping, between places and possibly even times; Changing, from one form into another; Binding, not just a broken bone but a broken spirit as well; and all the rest.

Perhaps, just perhaps . . . the psaltery would take on similar powers. Was it possible? Powers that I could wield on behalf of all Fincayra's peoples, with wisdom and grace not seen since the days of my grandfather.

I took a deep breath. Carefully, I lifted the little instrument in my hands, then slid the oaken bridge under the strings. A snap of my wrist—and it stood in place. I exhaled, knowing that the moment, my moment, was very near.

†HE MIRROR
OF MERLIN

Young Merlin is now stronger and wiser than ever, and his love for Hallia has blossomed fully. It is a richly beautiful springtime on Fincayra.

And then . . . everything changes. Merlin's precious sword—the one he will one day place in the stone to await King Arthur—is stolen. Searching madly for it, Merlin is lured to the most frightening place on the island: the Haunted Marsh, home of the terrible marsh ghouls. And to survive this quest, Merlin must also voyage to the most frightening place inside himself.

PROLOGUE

Many are the mirrors I have examined; many are the faces I have seen. Yet for all these years—lo, all these centuries—there is but one mirror, with one visage, I cannot forget. It has haunted me from the start, from that very first instant. And it haunts me no less to this day.

Mirrors, I assure you, can cause more pain than broadswords, more terror than ghouls.

Under the stone archway, mist billowed and swirled, roving about like an all-seeing eye.

The mist did not rise from the ground, or from some steaming pool nearby. Rather, this mist formed out of the very air under the arch, behind the strange, quivering curtain that held it back as a dam might hold a swelling tide. Even so, the vapors often pushed past, licking the purple-leafed vines that wrapped around the pillars. But more often, as now, they churned deep within the archway, forming and dissolving shapes in endless procession: ever changing, ever the same.

Then, without warning, the curtain of mist shuddered, hardening into a flat sheet. Beams of light struck its surface, breaking apart like shards of glass; vague shapes from the surrounding marshes reflected there. Somewhere behind the reflections, clouds continued to churn, touched by dark, distorted shadows. And a mysterious light, glinting from the depths beyond.

For this curtain was truly a mirror, one filled with mist—and more. A mirror with its own movement, its own pulse. A mirror with something stirring far beneath its surface.

Suddenly, from the very center came a waft of vapors, followed by something else—something slender. And twisted. And alive. Something very much like a hand.

With long nails, sharper than claws, the fingers reached outward, groping. Three of them, then a fourth, then a thumb. Wisps of mist from the marsh curled around them, adorning them with delicate, lacelike rings. But the fingers shook free before closing into a fist.

For a long moment, the fist squeezed itself tightly, as if testing its own reality. The skin, nearly as pale as the surrounding vapors, went whiter still. The fingernails dug deeper into the flesh. All over, the fist quivered from strain.

Ever so slowly, the hand started to relax. The fingers uncurled, flexed, and worked the air. Hazy threads wove themselves around the thumb and stretched across the open palm. At the same time, the mirror itself darkened. From the edges of the crumbling stones, deep shadows seeped inward, covering the surface. In a few moments, the whole archway gleamed like a black crystal, its smooth surface unbroken but for the pale hand squirming in its center.

A sharp creaking split the air. It might have come from the mirror, or the ancient stones themselves, or somewhere else entirely. With it came a scent—compellingly sweet, akin to rose blossoms.

A wind stirred, carrying away both the sound and the perfume. Both vanished into the rancid terrain of the Haunted Marsh. No one, not even the marsh ghouls themselves, noticed what had happened. Nor did anyone witness what happened next.

The hand, fingers splayed wide, lunged forward. Behind it came the wrist, forearm, and elbow. The gleaming surface suddenly shattered, melting back into a shifting, quivering mirror, as restless as the mists within its depths.

Out of the archway strode a woman. As she planted her boots on the muddy ground, she smoothed the creases on her white robe and silver-threaded shawl. Tall and slender she stood, with eyes as lightless as the interior of a stone. Glancing back at the mirror, she smiled grimly.

She gave her black, flowing locks a shake, and turned her attention to the marsh. For a long moment she listened to its distant wailing and hissing. Then she grunted in satisfaction. Under her breath, she whispered: "This time, my dear Merlin, you shall not elude me."

With that, she gathered her shawl about her shoulders and strode off into the gloom.

1

SHADOWS

I strained, throwing all my strength into the task, but my shadow refused to move.

Again I tried. Still, the stubborn shadow would not budge. Closing my eyes—a meaningless gesture, since they couldn't see anyway, having been replaced by my second sight over three years ago—I tried my best to concentrate. To perceive nothing but my shadow. That was not easy, on a bright summer day like this, though it still seemed easier than my task.

All right, then. Clearing my mind, I pushed aside the sound of rustling grasses on this alpine meadow, and of splattering streamwater nearby. No smells of springmint, or lavender, or pepperwort—almost strong enough to make me sneeze. No boulder, roughened by yellow lichens, resting beneath me; no mountains of Varigal, streaked with snow even in summer, rising above me. No wondering about whether I might encounter my old friend, the giant Shim, in these hills so near his home. And, most difficult of all, no drifting into thoughts about Hallia.

Just my shadow.

Starting from the bottom, I traced the shadow's outline on the grass. There were my boots, leather straps dangling, planted firmly on top of the boulder. Then my legs, hips, and chest, looking less scrawny than usual because of my billowing tunic. Protruding from one side, my leather satchel—and from the other, my sword. Next, my arms, bent with hands resting on hips. And my head, turned sideways just enough to show the tip of my nose, which, much to my consternation, had started to hook downward in recent months. Already more beak than nose, it reminded me of the hawk who had inspired my name. Then, of course, came my hair: even blacker than my shadow. And, I grumbled to myself, just as unruly.

Move, I commanded silently, all the while keeping my own body motionless.

No response.

Lift yourself, I intoned, focusing all my thoughts on the shadow's right arm.

Still no response.

I released a growl. Already I had wasted the entire morning trying to coax it to move independently. So what if shadow-working was a skill reserved only for the eldest wizards—true mages? I never was much good at waiting.

I drew a long, slow breath. *Lift. Lift, I say.*

For a long moment, I stared, exasperated, at the dark form. Then . . . something started to change. Slowly, very slowly, the shadow's outline started to quiver. The edges of its shoulders grew blurry, while its arms quaked so violently they seemed to swell in size.

Better. Much better. I forced myself not to move, not even to brush away the bothersome drops of perspiration rolling down my temples. *Now, right arm. Lift yourself.*

With a sharp jerk, the shadow's arm straightened. And lifted—all the way above the head. Though I held my own body fixed, a thrill raced through me—a mixture of excitement, and discovery, and pride in my growing powers. At last, I had done it! Worked my own shadow! I could hardly wait to show Hallia.

Though I felt as if I could fly off the boulder, I kept myself still. Only my widening grin betrayed my feelings. Returning my attention to the shadow, its arm still raised, I savored my success. To think that I, barely fifteen years of age, could move my shadow's—

Left arm? My whole chest constricted. It should have moved the right, not the left! With a roar, I stomped my boots and waved my own arms angrily. The shadow, as if in spite, did the same back at me.

"You foolish shadow! I'll teach you some obedience!"

"And when will that be?" asked a resonant voice behind me.

I spun around to face Hallia. Stepping as lightly as a doe, she seemed more supple than the summer grass. Yet I knew that, even in her young woman's form, she was ever alert to any possible danger—ready to run like the deer she could become in an instant. As the sunlight glinted on her auburn braid, her immense brown eyes watched me with humor. "Obedience, if I recall, isn't one of your strong points."

"Not me, my shadow!"

Her eyes sparkled mischievously. "Where leaps the stag, so leaps his shadow."

"But—but I . . ." My cheeks grew hotter as I stammered. "Why do you have to appear right now? Just when I've botched everything?"

She stroked her long chin. "If I didn't know better, I might think you had been hoping to impress me."

"Not at all." I clenched my fists, then shook them at my shadow. Seeing it wave its own fists back at me only made me angrier. "Fool shadow! I just want to make it do what it should."

Hallia bent to study a sprig of lupine, as deep purple as her robe. "And I just want to keep you a little humble." She sniffed the tower of petals. "That's usually Rhia's responsibility, but since she's off learning the speech of the canyon eagles—"

"With my horse to carry her," I grumbled, trying to stretch my stiff shoulders.

"True enough." She glanced up and smiled, more with her eyes than with her lips. "She can't, after all, run like a deer."

Something about her words, her tone, her smile, made my anger vanish like mist in the morning sun. Even my shoulders seemed to relax. How, I couldn't begin to explain. Yet all at once, I recalled the secrets she had shown me of transforming myself into a deer, as well as the joys of running beside her—with hooves instead of feet, four legs instead of two; with keen sight, and keener smell; with the ability to hear not just through my ears, but through my very bones.

"It's . . . well, it's—ahhh . . . ," I stammered. "Nice, I

suppose. To be here. With you, I mean. Just—well, just you."

Her doelike eyes, suddenly shy, turned aside.

Emboldened, I climbed down from the rock. "Even in these days, these weeks, we've been traveling together, we haven't had much time alone." Tentatively, I reached for her hand. "If it hasn't been one of your deer people, or some old friend, it's been—"

She jerked her hand away. "So you haven't liked what I've shown you?"

"No. I mean yes. That's . . . oh, that's not what I'm saying! You know how much I've loved being here—seeing your people's Summer Lands: those high meadows, the birthing hollow, all the hidden trails through the trees. It's just that, well, the best part has been . . ."

As my voice faltered, she cocked her head. "Yes?"

I glanced her way, meeting her gaze for barely an instant. But it was enough to make me forget what I had wanted to say.

"Yes?" she coaxed. "Tell me, young hawk."

"It's, well, been . . . Fumblefeathers, I don't know!" My brow furrowed. "Sometimes I envy old Cairpré, tossing off poems whenever he likes."

She half grinned. "These days, it's mostly love poems to your mother."

More flustered than ever, I exclaimed, "That's not what I meant!" Then, seeing her face fall, I realized my gaffe. "I mean . . . when I said that, what I meant was—not, well, not what I meant to say."

She merely shook her head.

Again, I stretched my hand toward her. "Please, Hallia. Don't judge me by my words."

"Hmfff," she grunted. "Then how should I judge you?"

"By something else."

"Like what?"

A sudden inspiration seized me. I grasped her hand, pulling her across the grass. Together we ran, our feet pounding in unison. As we neared the edge of the stream, our backs lowered, our necks lengthened, our arms stretched down to the ground. The bright green reeds by the water's edge, glistening with dew, bent before us. In one motion, one body it seemed, we sprang into the air, flowing as smoothly as the stream below us.

We landed on the opposite bank, fully transformed into deer. Swinging about, I reared back on my haunches and drew a deep breath, filling my nostrils with the rich aromas of the meadow—and the full-hearted freedom of a stag. Hallia's foreleg brushed against my own; I replied with a stroke of an antler along her graceful neck. An instant later we were bounding together through the grass, prancing with hooves high, listening to the whispering reeds and the many secret murmurs of the meadow. For a time measured not in minutes but in magic, we cavorted.

When, at last, we stopped, our tan coats shone with sweat. We trotted to the stream, browsed for a while on the shoots by the bank, then stepped lightly into the shallows. As we walked upstream, our backs lifted higher, our heads taller. Soon we were no longer wading with our hooves, but with our feet—mine booted, Hallia's bare.

In silence, we clambered up the muddy bank and stepped through the rushes. When we reached the boulder, scene of my unsuccessful shadow-working, Hallia faced me, her doe's eyes still alight. "I have something to tell you, young hawk. Something important."

I watched her, my heart pounding like a great hoof within my chest.

She started to speak, then caught herself. "It's—oh, it's so hard to put into words."

"I understand, believe me." Gently, I ran my finger down her arm. "Later perhaps."

Hesitantly, she tried again. "No, now. I've been wanting to say this for a while. And the feeling has grown stronger with every day we've spent in the Summer Lands."

"Yes?" I paused, trying to swallow. "What is it?"

She edged a bit closer. "I want you to, to . . . know something, young hawk."

"Know what?"

"That I . . . no, that you—"

Suddenly a heavy object rammed into me, knocking me over backward. I rolled across the grass, stopping only at the edge of the stream. After untangling myself from my tunic, which had somehow wrapped itself around my head and shoulders, I leaped to my feet with a spray of mud. Grimacing, I grasped the hilt of my sword and faced my attacker.

But instead of lunging forward, I groaned. "Not you. Not now."

A young dragon, her purple and scarlet scales aglow, sat beside us. She was tucking her leathery wings, still quivering from flight, against her back. Her immense, gangly form obscured the boulder, as well as a fair portion of the meadow, which is why she had sent me sprawling when she landed. Only Hallia's quick instincts had spared her the same fate.

The dragon drew a deep, ponderous breath. Her head,

nearly as large as my entire body, hung remorsefully from her huge shoulders. Even her wings drooped sadly, as did one of her blue, bannerlike ears. The other ear, as always, stuck straight out from the side of her head—looking less like an ear than a misplaced horn.

Hallia, seeing my angry expression, moved protectively to the dragon's side. She placed her hand on the end of the protruding ear. "Gwynnia's sorry, can't you see? She didn't mean any harm."

The dragon scrunched her nose and gave a deep, throaty whimper.

Hallia peered into her orange, triangular eyes. "She's only just learned to fly. Her landings are still a little clumsy."

"Little clumsy!" I fumed. "She might have killed me!"

I paced over to my staff, lying on the grass, and brandished it before the dragon's face. "You're as bad as a drunken giant. No, worse! At least he'd pass out eventually. You just keep getting bigger and clumsier by the day."

Gwynnia's eyes, glowing like lava, narrowed slightly. From deep within her chest, a rumble gathered, swelling steadily. The dragon suddenly stiffened and cocked her head, as if puzzled by the sound. Then, as the rumble faded away, she opened her gargantuan, teeth-studded jaws in a prolonged yawn.

"Be glad she hasn't learned yet how to breathe fire," cautioned Hallia. Quickly, she added, "Though I'm sure she'd never use it on a friend." She scratched the edge of the rebellious ear. "Would you, Gwynnia?"

The dragon gave a loud snort. Then, from the other end of the meadow, the barbed end of her tail lifted, curled, and moved swiftly closer. With the grace of a butterfly, the remotest tip of the tail alighted on Hallia's shoulder. There it rested, purple scales upon purple cloth, squeezing her gently.

Brushing some of the mud from my tunic, I gave an exasperated sigh. "It's hard to stay angry at either of you for long." I gazed into one of the dragon's bright eyes. "Forgive me, will you? I forgot—just for a moment—that you're never far from Hallia's side."

The young woman turned toward me. "For just a moment," she said softly, "I, too, forgot."

I nodded sadly. "It's no fault of yours."

"Oh, but it is." She stroked the golden scales of the barbed tail. "When I started singing to her in the evenings, all those songs I learned as a child, I had no idea she would grow so attached."

"Or so large."

Hallia nearly smiled. "I suppose we should never have let Cairpré give her such a weighty name, out of ancient dragon-lore, unless we expected her to live up to it someday."

"That's right—the name of the first queen of the dragons, mother of all their race." I chewed my lip, recalling the old legend. "The one who risked her own life to swallow the fire from a great lava mountain, so that she, and all her descendants, might also breathe flames."

At that, Gwynnia opened wide her jaws and gave another yawn, this time so loud that we both had to cover our ears. When at last the yawn ended, I observed, "Seems like the queen may need a nap." In a hopeful whisper, I added, "We may get to finish our conversation yet."

Hallia nodded, even as she shifted uneasily. But before

she could say anything, a new sound sliced through the air. It was a high, mournful keening—the kind of sound that could only come from someone in the throes of death. Or, more accurately, someone for whom death itself would be a reprieve.

THE WINGS
OF MERLIN

Merlin's old enemy, Rhita Gawr, plans to invade Fincayra, overwhelming Merlin's homeland with an army of deathless creatures from the Otherworld.

Merlin will need every friend he has made in his past adventures to save the land he loves. He must also solve the mystery of his people's lost wings. And in the end he will be required to make a great sacrifice—one befitting the great wizard he has become. Fincayra will be saved, though not in the way anyone could have expected. And Merlin's life will never be the same.

Available in paperback from Ace Books in November 2002.

PROLOGUE

Wings, take me back! How often have I dreamed, in the centuries since that day, of returning to that place and time, of facing once again the choice that changed everything.

Such longing, though, is useless. An idea that is lost may yet be reborn, but a day that is lost is gone forever. And even if I could return, would I choose any differently? Probably not. Yet how can I be certain? Even after all these years, I know so very little.

But there is one thing I do know, a gift of that long ago day: Wings are far more than feathered arms. They are part mystery—and also part miracle. For what bears high the body may also give flight to the soul.

Bare feet in the water, the boy sat alone.

Though his sandy hair spun in jovial curls, his eyes, as

brown as the muddy tarn before him, seemed strangely sad. Not that he minded being alone. As far back as he could recall—most of his eight or nine years—he'd lived that way. Even when others welcomed him at their meal table, offered him a pallet of straw for a night's rest, or shared their games with him, he knew his only real companion was solitude.

His life was simple—just like his name, Lleu. Whether the name had come from his parents before they died, or from someone else he'd met in his travels, he didn't know. And why should it matter? His name was just a word. A sound. Nothing more.

He plucked a reed, ran his finger down the shaft as if it were a tiny spear, and tossed it at a dead leaf floating in the water. A perfect hit: The leaf sank under the weight, sending rings of tiny ripples across the tarn. As the water lapped at his toes, the boy almost smiled.

Then, seeing that his spear had dislodged a small, lavender-backed beetle, he leaned forward. The little insect flailed, trying without success to work its sopping wings in the water. In a few seconds, it would drown. The boy stretched out his leg, caught the beetle on his toe, and brought it safely to shore.

"There ye be, friend." Taking the tiny creature in his hand, he blew gently on its wings. "Jest a bit o' sunshine an' ye'll be flyin' again."

Almost in answer, the beetle shivered and lifted into the air, flying haphazardly. It veered toward the boy's head. With a moist tap, it landed on top of his ear, then crawled onto one of his dangling curls.

"Likes me, do ye?"

Chuckling, the boy turned back to the tarn. This was

one of his favorite places to camp, whenever his wanderings brought him to this part of Fincayra. Even now, as the days shortened and ice choked many streams, the water here still burbled freely. More than once, he'd caught a pheasant here, or made supper from the brambleberries lining the water's edge. And it was quiet, far from any roads, and the rascally knaves he sometimes met there.

Met—though not for long. He could outrun any of them. He could run for a whole day without stopping if necessary. Lifting one foot out of the water, he studied its calluses, as thick and rough as the leather on an old boot. But even better. These soles wouldn't wear out. All they needed was a tarn like this, for soaking after a long day's trek.

Lleu's face tightened. He scanned the wintry sky, watching the gray, leaden clouds slide above the leafless trees on the far side of the tarn. Turning back to his foot, he knew he'd really welcome a pair of boots, or sandals at least, in the colder days to come. Days when he might need to cross long stretches of snow to find his next meal.

To be sure, being an orphan had some advantages. He could roam wherever he pleased, sleep wherever he liked. The sky above was his ceiling, often brightly painted. Meals came at odd times, but at least they usually came. He expected little, and normally got it. And yet . . . he longed for something more. Placing his foot back in the cool, dark waters of the tarn, tinted red from the leaves still clinging to the bramble bushes, he thought about another place and time—a time too distant for memory, yet impossible to forget.

He couldn't recall her name. Nor even her face. The color of her eyes, the shape of her mouth, the length of her hair—all lay hidden, buried deeper than his dreams. He didn't know her name, or the sound of her voice. He wasn't even sure she was his mother.

But he remembered her smell. Earthy, like fallen leaves; tangy, like rose hips in summer; zesty, more than meadowsweet.

She had held him, that much he knew. Every so often, sitting by a tarn like this one, he might hear a blackbird warbling, and the wind humming through the reeds. And then he'd feel sure that she had sung to him, too. Yes, she had! What sort of song, in what sort of tones, he couldn't say. Yet he knew she'd held him close, singing softly, surrounding him with her fragrant skin.

He shuddered. Probably, he told himself, it was just a sudden chill in the air. Sunlight felt weaker at this time of the year, and the wind harsher. Already a tracery of ice lined the far side of the tarn. The longest nights of the year, he knew, lay just ahead.

But he'd survived other winters, at least five or six, and he'd survive this one, as well. Tomorrow he'd move farther south, closer to the coast. Meadows there stayed mostly unfrozen, and if snow fell, it rarely lasted for more than a day or two. As long as he didn't venture too close to the sea, and that shoreline where the dark mist swirled endlessly, forming twisted shapes and scary faces, he'd be fine.

A fire. That's what he needed now. He reached into the pocket of his tunic, squeezing some shavings of dry bark, as well as the pair of iron stones that never failed to spark a flame. He would warm himself, as well as the strip of dried beef a man had kindly tossed him that morning, and make camp for the night.

Lleu stood, scanning the bank as he slapped his feet on the mud. He knew from experience the weight and thickness of the sticks he needed for a good fire: several as thin as his smallest finger, a load or two of larger ones, and at least one about the size of his leg. Dry kindling was more tricky to find, especially at this time of year, which was why he always carried some. Otherwise he might have to use a strip of cloth from his tunic. And burning his tunic was burning his blanket.

Behind the brambles, he spied the largest branch he would need, ripped from a hawthorn tree by some heavy wind. He ran over. But the branch weighed more than he'd thought—too heavy to carry, or even drag. Nonetheless, he tried, tugging on it with all his weight. Still it wouldn't budge.

"All right then," he muttered aloud, "I'll bust ye! All I'm needin' is 'nuf to burn."

Bracing his foot against a cracked portion of the branch, he grabbed the upper end. Hard as he could, he pulled. The branch wriggled, creaking slightly, but didn't break. Again he tried, without success.

"Jest break now, will ye?"

As the boy set his hands to try again, a sword suddenly slashed through the air. The blade severed the branch, as if it were nothing more than a twig. A section just the right size to carry rolled on the muddy ground.

Grateful as well as startled, the boy whirled around. But his words of thanks caught in his throat. There, facing him, stood the most fearsome warrior he had ever seen—a man, immensely tall and sturdy, wearing a horned skull as a mask. Behind the mask shone wrathful eyes. And worse, the warrior carried two massive swords, each strapped to one of his arms.

Strange, thought the boy. *Those swords* . . . He sucked in his breath. They weren't, he suddenly realized, strapped to the man's arms. Rather, they *were* his arms, bound somehow to the warrior's powerful shoulders.

The masked man stared down at him. In a deep but hollow voice that seemed to echo from somewhere far-away, he commanded, "Tell me your name, boy."

"Ah, 'tis . . . Lleu, m-master." He tried to swallow, but his throat only made the sound of a whimper. "Least that's what I be mostly called."

"Have you no home?"

"N-no, master."

"Have you no parents?"

"N-no, master."

The warrior laughed mirthlessly, even as one of his swordlike arms lifted. "Then, young whelp, you shall be my first victim."

1

THREADS

This wasn't just a familiar stroll down a wooded path. No, this was something far different: more like a flight.

Luminous threads of light wove through the loom of branches, making the forest floor sparkle. The springy turf, softened by centuries of fallen leaves, seemed to lift me higher with every step. I felt I could leap into the trees, or sail like the golden butterflies among their branches. I had taken this woodland path many times before, to be sure. But it had never seemed at once so bright and so dark, so full of clarity as well as mystery.

Hallia, her hand in mine, walked with the same lilt in her step—and something more, the added grace of a deer. She knew, with every curl of her toe and sweep of her arm, the simple glory of motion. Truly, she *was* motion, as fluid as the falling leaf that spun downward from the highest boughs, as gentle as the forest breeze that stroked her auburn hair.

I smiled, thinking of the many such walks we had taken in the past few months. When she had first invited me to live among her people and learn their ways, several of the elders of her clan had objected. Long councils and fierce debates ensued. I was, after all, not a member of the Mellwyn-bri-Meath. And worse, I was a man. How could they possibly trust me with some of their most precious secrets, when my kind had so often hunted and killed their own, for no better reason than hunger for a slab of venison?

Hallia, in the end, had prevailed. The tales of how I'd saved her life didn't sway the elders, nor even the things I'd accomplished for the land of Fincayra. No, it was something far more simple, and powerful: Hallia's love for me. Faced with that, even the most skeptical members of her clan finally gave way. And so, in the time since, I'd learned how to drink water from the rill without disturbing its flow, how to feel the ground as if it were part of my own body, and how to hear with the openness of the air itself.

Such walks we had taken! Hallia guided me through meadows where ancient trails lay hidden, through tall stands of eelgrass that could be woven into baskets or clothing, and through secret glades where many a fawn-child had been born. Often we strode upright, as we did now. Just as often, we ran side by side as doe and stag, our bodies sailing above the soil more than treading upon it.

Yet on this day and on this trail, I felt closer to her than ever before. Tonight, when we reached the far side of the forest, I would show her a secret of my own—my stargazing stone. And there I would give her the present I'd been saving. I tapped my leather satchel in anticipation, knowing that in many ways the gift belonged to her already.

Seeing a stream just ahead, I lifted my staff so it wouldn't catch on the gooseberry brambles along the bank. Then, without a word, we leaped into the air, our four legs springing in unison as if they belonged to a single person. Beneath us, the water sparkled, its surface alive with light, even where it passed under a branch or over a moss-splattered stone. We landed gently on the opposite side and continued down the path.

I gazed about, my second sight—now sharper and truer than my lost eyesight had ever been—overwhelmed by the wide array of highlights and colors. Even the etchings on my staff seemed to glimmer with the magic surrounding us. Dew glistened on rain-washed limbs, while the forest floor shone orange, scarlet, and brown. Above our heads, a pair of squirrels, their eyes nearly as large as their bulging cheeks, scurried over a branch, chattering ceaselessly. Beech trees' smooth bark reflected the sun like mirrors, and linden leaves trembled like running streams. Clumps of moss, deep green flecked with red, nestled among the burly roots of oaks and pines, often joined by parades of yellow toadstools.

Resins wafted everywhere—from the needles of fir trees, sweeter than honeysuckle; from rainwater cupped in palmate leaves, as rich in smells as marshland pools; and from fallen branches already more soil than wood. I could smell, not far away, the gamey scent of a fox's den. And I knew that the fox itself could smell us approaching.

The sound of the stream behind us merged with the undulating whisper of wind among the branches. And, as always, I heard in the forest wind many distinct voices: the deep sighing of oak, the crackling of ash, the rhythmic whooshing of pine. Many voices, yes—and one above all, the unified breath of the living forest.

A place of many wonders. Those words, the first description I'd ever heard of Fincayra, never felt so true as today. Especially here, in the depths of Druma Wood. Even the harsh winds of winter, which had already brought snow and frost to much of the rest of Fincayra, seemed unable to penetrate here. Though some forest animals had retreated to their burrows and hollow logs, and many trees had changed to brown and tan, the Druma still pulsed with life.

And that wasn't all that set this forest apart. Much of Fincayra still suffered from the long years of suspicion, even hatred, that divided its many races and kept them separate from one another—and especially from the race of men and women. But not here. Even during Stangmar's Blight, when creatures in other parts of the island feared to show themselves in daylight, this place remained at peace. Here, someone's good fortune also gave strength to others; one creature's loss brought widespread grief. It was truly a community.

Hallia squeezed my hand, halting us both. Following her gaze, I spied an extraordinary bird perched on a branch above our heads. There was no mistaking the bright purple crest on its head, nor the flaming scarlet feathers along its tail. An alleah bird! For a breathless moment, the creature watched us in silence, cocking its head pensively. Then, with a dazzling flash of iridescence, it flew off into the forest and disappeared.

"The long-tailed alleah bird," whispered Hallia. "A sign of good luck."

At that instant, something slammed into my back, sending me sprawling into a stand of hip-high ferns. I tumbled through the stalks, finally smacking into a boulder. Head spinning, I crawled free of the ferns. With effort, I straightened my leather satchel, which had wrapped itself around my neck, retrieved my staff, and started to regain my feet.

"Greetings, Brother." Rhia, dressed in a suit of tightly woven vines, placed her hands upon her hips and laughed heartily. "You're still my favorite place to land."

"Sure," I groaned. "But great seasons! Need you always land so hard?"

She reached down and tugged on my arm to help me stand. "Well, you might not notice me otherwise." She paused to give Hallia a knowing wink. "Occupied as you are with the world of romance."

Hallia's face flushed as red as the leaves of wild geranium by her feet. "Rhia!"

"Haka-haka-tikky-tichhh," cackled a tiny creature who had poked his head out of the leafy pocket on Rhia's sleeve. His small, furred head bobbed with laughter, causing his long ears to flap against the sides of his face. Meanwhile, his lopsided grin opened wide, revealing only three teeth, all of them as green as his eyes.

"Haka-haka-tichhh. Poor lover manman!" cried the beast, speaking in a rapid, squeaky voice, almost too fast for me to catch his words. "Lost his wittywits, he has. Now his balance, too! Haaa-ha-haka-tch."

I glowered at him. "Quiet there, skinny ears! Or I'll—"

Hallia stepped over and touched her finger to my lips. "Hush, now. He's just a scullyrumpus, and they're all endless pranksters. He can't help himself, young hawk."

Hearing her use my familiar name, I suddenly relaxed. As I looked into her wide brown eyes, as deep as magical pools, I forgot my anger. All I could think of was the woman beside me, the woman I loved. Slowly, I leaned closer, ready to . . .

"Kissiesnug! Kissiesnug!" exclaimed the beast, flapping his oversized ears. "No more words for clumsy manman. Just kissies! Haka-haka-hakakakak."

Straightening myself, I glared at Rhia. "Why do you keep that little pest around?"

She watched me with amusement, even as she scratched his furry neck. "Scully? Oh, we have lots in common. He's part of the forest, like me. And a tree dweller, like me."

"And totally disrespectful," I added.

She nodded. "Also like me."

Despite myself, I grinned. "All right. But can't you stop landing on me like that?"

"Why? It keeps you humble."

To my dismay, Hallia herself smiled.

"Keeps me bruised and broken!" I roared.

"Oo-cha-oooo-cha," squeaked the beast, waving his paws in mock terror. "Now clumsy man veryveryvery angry." To Rhia, he cried, "Better go now. Next time he fallfalls, could be on us!"

He clutched his sides, cackling so merrily he almost fell out of the pocket. "You too, deersister," he called to

Hallia. "Run away fast, ha-chhh-ha-chhh. Fast as hoofy-feet will carry you!"

This was too much for me. "Enough, Scullyrumpus." I brandished my staff. "One more insult and I'll turn you into the worm you really are."

Instead of shrinking back into the pocket in fear, as I'd expected, he simply scowled back at me. "Scullyrumpus Eiber y Findalair to you," he piped. "Think you cannycan use first name only? A cheeky little manman you are."

"Cheeky!" I exclaimed, my temples pounding. "You dare call *me* cheeky?"

Rhia raised her hand. "Hold, Merlin." She glanced down at the beast on her sleeve. "And you, Scully. It's too lovely a day for this." To emphasize the point, she gave her head a shake, tossing her brown curls. "Come now, Brother. You can join me."

"Join you?"

"Yes. I'm learning to fly."

I glared at her. "You'll have to sprout wings first."

"Not that way, you fool." She rubbed her hands on her leafy thighs, wiping away any moisture. Then she secured to her belt the small orange globe that sometimes, as now, showed no light, but other times glowed without any warning: the Orb of Fire. Her care, I knew, was justified, for like the other legendary Treasures of Fincayra, the Orb held great power—and even greater mystery. Ready at last, she reached for one of the thick vines dangling nearby. Then she announced, with great confidence, "This way."

Her furry companion nodded, ears flapping. At the same time, he shrank deeper into the pocket.

Wrapping her hands and feet around the vine, Rhia uttered something in the low, rustling tongue of a hemlock. Instantly, the tree behind her straightened its trunk, lifting the vine and her with it. Again she spoke a command, and the vine whipped suddenly, hurling her through the canopy of branches. Hallia and I gasped in unison as she let go, spun twice through the air, then grabbed hold of another vine. This time she swung a wide arc, showering us with needles and twigs. Again she released, flipped over, and spread her arms outward like a pair of wings. For a split second, she hung there, resting on nothing but air.

Hallia clutched my arm. "She's going to fall!"

I stiffened, my mind racing. Should I make a gust of wind? Another vine?

Before I could do anything, the hemlock tree swept itself around. A long, wide-limbed branch reached out and caught Rhia bodily, bouncing with her weight. Swiftly, the tree lowered her. Just above the ground, she rolled free, twirled in the air, and landed gently on her feet, smiling broadly. She stood before us, stroking the bulge on her sleeve where Scullyrumpus had withdrawn.

Hallia sighed. "Rhia, you are truly a herd of one."

"Thanks," she replied, working back into her hair the dressing of leaves that had come loose. "Care to try?"

Hallia's round eyes shone with amusement. "No, no. Unlike those of you who crave those wings you lost so long ago, we deer-folk have no need to fly."

"Once you took a ride on the back of your dragon friend," Rhia reminded her.

"That was Gwynnia's idea, not mine! I jumped off the first instant I could."

Rhia faced me. "How about you then, Merlin? Are you

willing to try?" Sensing my hesitation, she added, "Or will that stubble on your chin have to grow into a full-length beard before you have enough courage?"

Hallia glanced at me worriedly. "Don't, young hawk."

"I've no lack of courage," I declared, rubbing my chin.

"Just—just intelligence," said a muffled voice in Rhia's sleeve.

"Quiet, now," barked Rhia. "Let him try." Turning back to me, she said, "Now, here's how you—"

Ignoring her, I tossed aside my staff, unbuckled my sword, and reached for the vine. Brusquely, I spoke my own rustling phrase. To my own surprise, the vine jumped upward, carrying me aloft. Wind rushed by my face, streaming my black locks of hair, fluttering the sleeves of my tunic. Feeling my confidence swell, I spoke again, and the vine swung around the hemlock's trunk, slicing graceful curves through the air. Over limbs and under I sailed, as free as a soaring hawk.

Flush with the joy of flight, I called once more to the tree. A new vine whipped to my side. At the highest point of my arc, I cast the old vine aside and leaped to grasp the new one. For several heartbeats I floated high above the ground, feeling like a creature of the wind itself. Even as I reached for the vine, its supple length wrapped around my hands and feet.

Holding tight to the vine, I plummeted downward, ready for the sudden tensing that I knew would hurl me high into the boughs again. Lack of courage, indeed! Rhia should know better by now. Down, down, down, I sped, watching the whirl of green and brown.

Craaack! My back rammed into a spiky lower branch, snapping it off completely. A rustling howl arose from the tree. My vine jerked violently, shaking me loose. I hurtled through open air, flying straight into the same patch of ferns where I'd landed when Rhia first arrived. With a thud, I hit the ground, rolling through the ferns and smacking into the boulder again.

It was all I could do to lift my head, and then only for a moment. I slumped back into the stalks. My entire body ached, especially the tender spot between my shoulder blades. With supreme effort, I tried to stand, but a new spell of dizziness struck and I collapsed again.

Hallia and Rhia rushed over. Together, they dragged me out of the ferns and helped me stretch out on the soft turf of the path. Pulling a mass of torn fronds from my mouth, I could only sputter, "What . . . happened?"

Hallia merely shook her head. Rhia, for once, said nothing. Even the little terror in her pocket remained silent, probably because he knew he was within my reach.

"I guess flying," I said groggily, "takes more than courage."

At that, the hemlock twitched abruptly. From high among its branches, a single cone fell, plunking me on the forehead.

As I groaned, Rhia bobbed her head. "Right," she agreed. "Much more."